Touch the Moon

A traditional tale

First published in 2004 by
Franklin Watts
338 Euston Road
London
NW1 3BH

Franklin Watts Australia
Level 17 / 207 Kent Street
Sydney
NSW 2000

A CIP catalogue record for this book is available
from the British Library.

ISBN 978 0 7496 5780 2

Series Editor: Jackie Hamley
Series Advisors: Dr Barrie Wade, Dr Hilary Minns
Design: Peter Scoulding

Printed in China

Franklin Watts is a division of
Hachette Children's Books,
an Hachette Livre UK company.
www.hachettelivre.co.uk

READING CORNER

Touch the Moon

Retold by
Carrie Weston

Illustrated by
Gwyneth Williamson

W
FRANKLIN WATTS
LONDON•SYDNEY

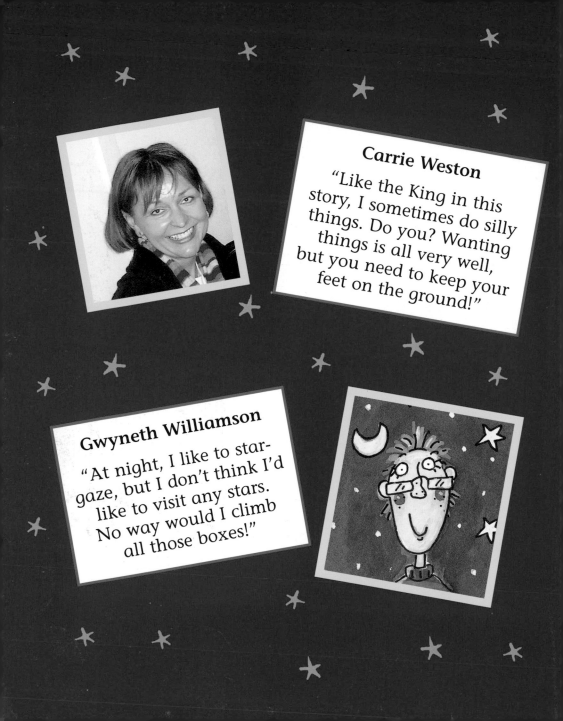

Carrie Weston

"Like the King in this story, I sometimes do silly things. Do you? Wanting things is all very well, but you need to keep your feet on the ground!"

Gwyneth Williamson

"At night, I like to star-gaze, but I don't think I'd like to visit any stars. No way would I climb all those boxes!"

The King looked up at the Moon.

It was round and shiny
and beautiful.

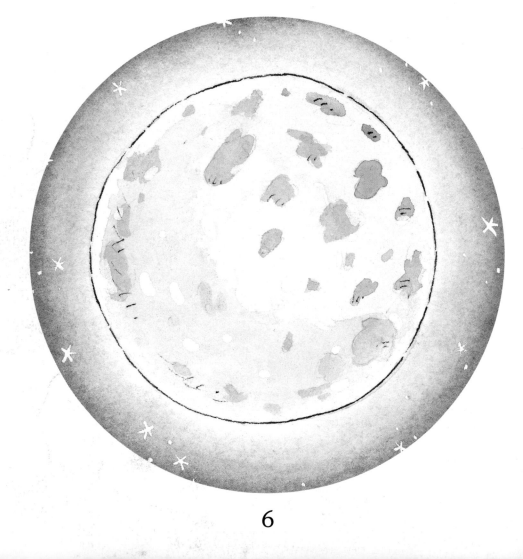

The King longed to touch it.

Then the King had an idea.

9

"Boxes!" yelled the King.

"Bring me boxes!"

The King began to make a tower.

He put one box
on top of another ...

... and another ...

... and another.

Still the Moon
was far away.

"More boxes!" called down the King.

Soon the tower reached
far up into the sky.

Still the King could not touch the Moon.

"More boxes!" called down the King.

But there were no more boxes.

The King had an idea: "Take a box from the bottom of the tower and I'll put it on the top!"

The King looked up at the Moon and rubbed his sore head.

Notes for parents and teachers

READING CORNER has been structured to provide maximum support for new readers. The stories may be used by adults for sharing with young children. Primarily, however, the stories are designed for newly independent readers, whether they are reading these books in bed at night, or in the reading corner at school or in the library.

Starting to read alone can be a daunting prospect. READING CORNER helps by providing visual support and repeating words and phrases, while making reading enjoyable. These books will develop confidence in the new reader, and encourage a love of reading that will last a lifetime!

If you are reading this book with a child, here are a few tips:

1. Make reading fun! Choose a time to read when you and the child are relaxed and have time to share the story.

2. Encourage children to reread the story, and to retell the story in their own words, using the illustrations to remind them what has happened.

3. Give praise! Remember that small mistakes need not always be corrected.

READING CORNER covers three grades of early reading ability, with three levels at each grade. Each level has a certain number of words per story, indicated by the number of bars on the spine of the book, to allow you to choose the right book for a young reader:

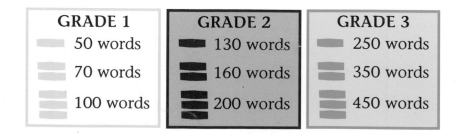

GRADE 1	GRADE 2	GRADE 3
50 words	130 words	250 words
70 words	160 words	350 words
100 words	200 words	450 words